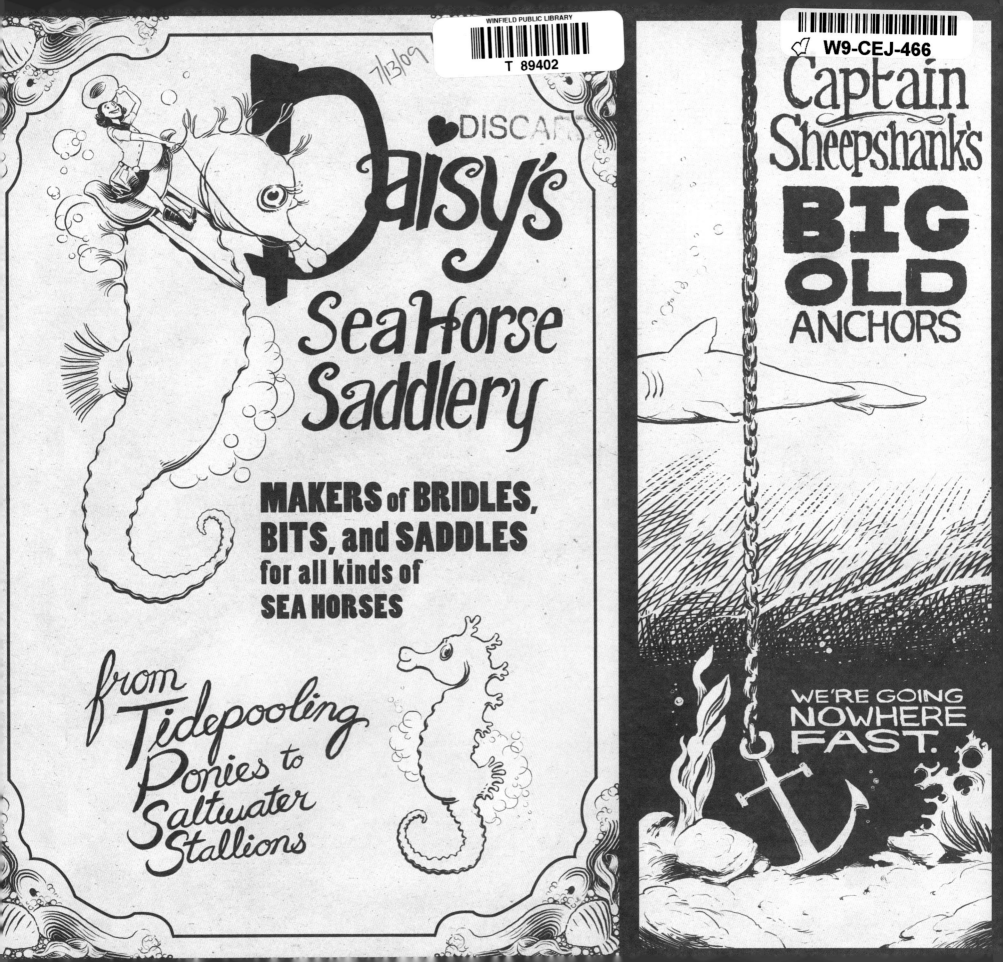

"B.T.*a.h.*B.W.P."
or
"A Cetacean *of a* Tale"

BILLY TWIT
BLUE WHA

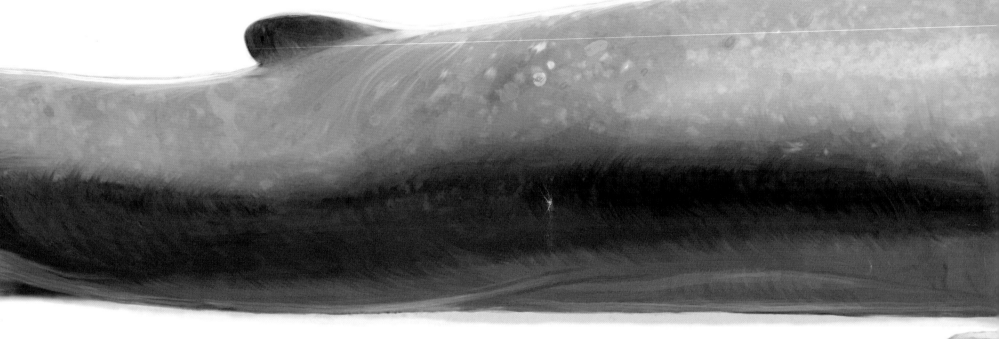

MAC BARNETT
AUTHOR

ADAM REX
ILLUSTRATOR

TERS and his
LE PROBLEM

D𝒾sney ★ HYPERION BOOKS

NEW YORK

This story is for Jon. If it weren't for Jon, this story
wouldn't be.

—MB

I was going to dedicate it to Jon. Now what am I gonna do,
dedicate another book to my wife? Like she still notices.

—AR

First Edition

10 9 8 7 6 5 4 3 2 1

Printed in Singapore

Reinforced binding

Library of Congress Cataloging-in-Publication Data on file.

ISBN 978-0-7868-4958-1

Visit www.hyperionbooksforchildren.com

Mom says:

. . .

But I'm not worried. See, I know a thing or two about blue whales.

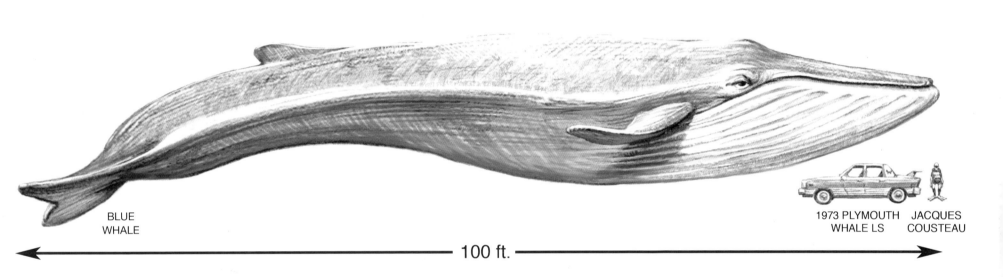

BLUE
WHALE

1973 PLYMOUTH   JACQUES
WHALE LS   COUSTEAU

100 ft.

I mean, they're the biggest animals in the world, ever. It's not like
you can just have one delivered to your house overnight.

"That's not just any blue whale, Billy. That's *your* blue whale. And it's your responsibility to take him wherever you go. Now, hurry up and get moving."

There's absolutely no way she's getting me to take that whale to school.

When I get to school, I try to hide my blue whale; but my teacher, Mr. Wembley, notices him.

"Oh my!" he says. "Bless my barnacles. A *Balaenoptera musculus*! Oh, Billy, you must bring this fabulous creature into our classroom!"

This is
not going
well.

Today Mr. Wembley was supposed to show us a movie about cowboys. Instead, he lectures about blue whales.

"Now, listen up, kiddos. Did you know that instead of teeth, blue whales have baleen? It's like a giant comb that traps food inside their mouths. And it's made out of the same stuff as our fingernails!"

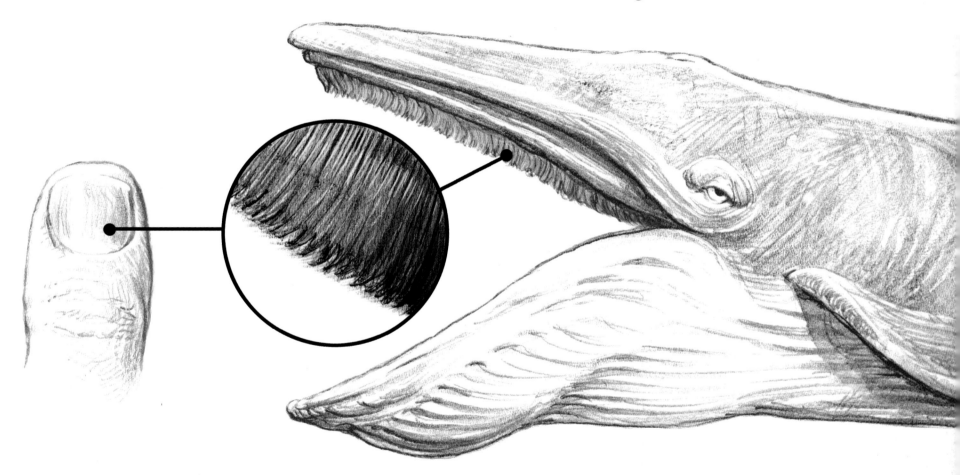

"Gross," someone says.

"What about the cowboy movie?" says someone else. "This is your fault, Billy Twitters."

Alexis Winters-Pierce, whose hair smells like tangerines, hands out party invitations right before recess.

"Hey, Billy," she says, "I'm having a pool party on Saturday. You should come."

"Great!" I say. "But I'll have to bring my blue whale along. That's fine, right?"

"Your whale can't fit in my pool! Sorry, Billy. You're uninvited."

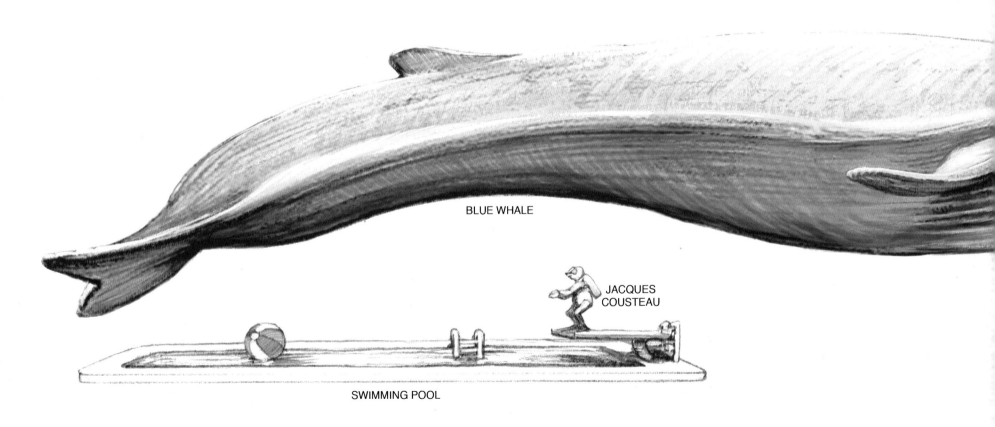

BLUE WHALE

JACQUES COUSTEAU

SWIMMING POOL

Recess. Frank Grunner taps me on the shoulder with a meaty finger. Frank always smells like corn chips, even when he hasn't been eating them.

"Hey, Twitters," says Frank, "that blue whale is the stupidest pet I've ever seen. Why didn't you get a cool animal, like a dinosaur or something?"

Everyone on the playground laughs.

BLUE
WHALE

DINOSAUR
(CAMARASAURUS)

"This blue whale is better than a dinosaur, Frank. It can be underwater for an hour without taking a breath. I don't think anything alive millions of years ago could do that."

Frank looks stumped.

But then Tilbie Peel, the class know-it-all, speaks up. "Actually, Billy, scientists believe that the plesiosaur could dive for two hours without surfacing for air. And then, of course, there was the *Carcharodon megalodon*, a giant prehistoric shark that pretty much spent its entire life underwater."

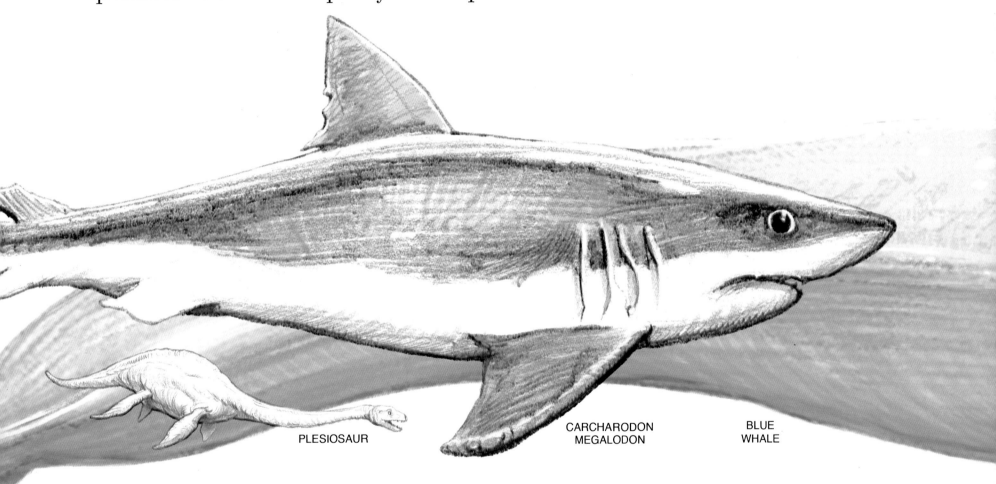

PLESIOSAUR

CARCHARODON
MEGALODON

BLUE
WHALE

"Yeah," says Frank. "You forgot about the *Carcharodon megalodon*, didn't you, Twitters?"

On most days, Frank Grunner locks Tilbie Peel in the girls' bathroom. Today he picks Tilbie first for his kickball team.

Nobody picks me. Or my whale.

After school, the bus breaks down. I'm trying to sneak my whale past everybody when Mr. Whitbread, the bus driver, sees me. "Hey, Billy," he says. "Could you give these kids a ride home on your whale?"

"I'd rather not," I say.

"All aboard!" says Mr. Whitbread.

The kids get on my whale. I get on my bike. But I haven't even pedaled out of the parking lot when I hear someone scream.

"Stop this whale!" shouts Mr. Whitbread. "Call the fire department!"

I look up.

Tilbie Peel is stuck in the blowhole.

How was your day at school?

my dad asks when I finally get home.

"Horrible," I tell him as I head upstairs.

"Not so fast, young man," he says.

"You've got some responsibilities."

"Responsibilities?" I ask.

"That's right. According to the *Blue Whale Owner's Manual* . . .

YOU'VE GOT TO

WASH YOUR WHALE,

"wrestle your whale, race your whale, and take your whale to the park."

It's almost dark when I finish. Just as I'm crawling into bed, Mom says, "Billy, you've got a blue whale to feed."

It turns out blue whales don't eat baked peas—I tried those. The manual says they eat krill—tiny shrimp things that they find by gulping ten-thousand-gallon mouthfuls of seawater.

"Dad," I ask, "where can I find ten thousand gallons of seawater?"

My dad looks up from the television. "Try the sea."

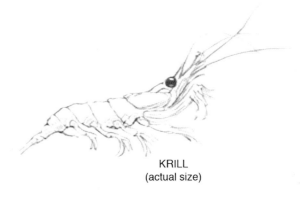

KRILL
(actual size)

The sea is cold. It's cold and wet, and it looks like it's trying to eat the dock. There's an old boat captain just watching me, grinning.

"Ahoy, there," says the captain. "That's a lot of water for a wee boy like you. If I didn't know better, I'd say you were feeding a blue whale!"

He starts laughing. I don't find his joke very funny.

And so here I am.

Let me tell you this: the inside of a whale's mouth stinks. It smells the way sweaty gym socks smell when they haven't been washed for weeks. Unwashed, sweaty gym socks that have been worn by a fish. A sweaty, stinking fish.

The stink is so bad that I'm considering running away to Montana. Then I realize:

In here, nobody's telling me to wash my whale.

In here, nobody's laughing at my whale.

In here, there's plenty of room for a bed.

So I
move
in.

Sometimes the only way to escape from the problems caused by your blue whale is to spend some time *inside* your blue whale. As long as I brush and floss his baleen a few times a day, it's a pretty pleasant place to be.

And best of all, a room this big never looks messy.